Fun Pet Stories

My Guinea Pig Is Funny

Myrna Nau

illustrated by
Aurora Aguilera

PowerKiDS press.

New York

Published in 2019 by The Rosen Publishing Group, Inc.
29 East 21st Street, New York, NY 10010

First Edition

Editor: Elizabeth Krajnik
Art Director: Michael Flynn
Book Design: Raúl Rodriguez
Illustrator: Aurora Aguilera

Cataloging-in-Publication Data

Names: Nau, Myrna.
Title: My guinea pig is funny / Myrna Nau.
Description: New York : PowerKids Press, 2019. | Series: Fun pet stories | Includes index.
Identifiers: ISBN 9781538345962 (pbk.) | ISBN 9781538344873 (library bound) | ISBN 9781538345979 (6pack)
Subjects: LCSH: Guinea pigs—Juvenile fiction. | Pets—Juvenile fiction.
Classification: LCC PZ7.N38 My 2019 | DDC [E]—dc23

Manufactured in the United States of America

CPSIA Compliance Information: Batch #CWPK19. For further information contact Rosen Publishing, New York, New York at 1-800-237-9932

Contents

My name is Miranda.

This is my pet guinea pig, Griswold.

4

We got Griswold
from an animal shelter.

He doesn't get along with other guinea pigs.

Griswold is silly!
He hides in his towel tent.

8

I peek at him in there.

Griswold has big front teeth!

He chews on wood to keep his teeth
healthy. Griswold is a noisy chewer!

I take Griswold outside.

Griswold loves to chase after me! He's really fast!

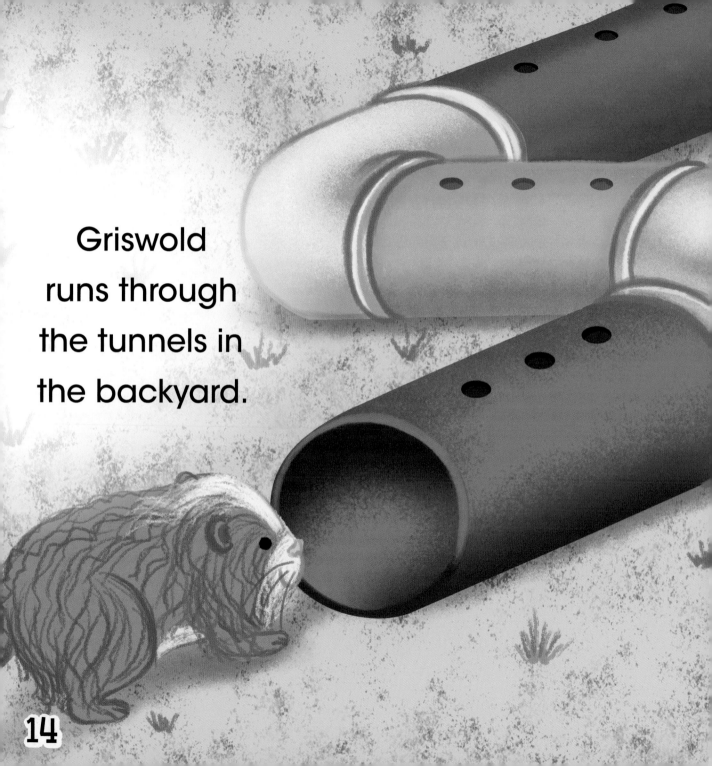

Griswold
runs through
the tunnels in
the backyard.

14

He pops in and out!

Griswold makes lots of funny sounds.

When
he's hungry,
Griswold
wheeks!

17

Griswold makes a purring sound
when I pet him.

Sometimes he growls when he's upset.

Griswold popcorns when he's excited. He jumps straight up in the air.

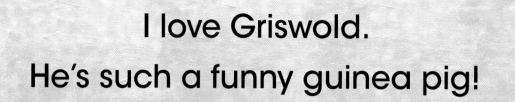

I love Griswold.
He's such a funny guinea pig!

Words to Know

animal shelter

teeth

tunnel

Index